THE INCREDIBLE DIARY OF...

Amazing Adventures

Edited By Jess Giaffreda

First published in Great Britain in 2019 by:

Young Writers
Remus House
Coltsfoot Drive
Peterborough
PE2 9BF
Telephone: 01733 890066
Website: www.youngwriters.co.uk

Foreword

Dear Reader,

You will never guess what I did today! Shall I tell you? Some primary school pupils wrote some diary entries and I got to read them, and they were EXCELLENT!

They wrote them in school and sent them to us here at Young Writers. We'd given their teachers some bright and funky worksheets to fill in, and some fun and fabulous (and free) resources to help spark ideas and get inspiration flowing.

And it clearly worked because WOW!! I can't believe the adventures I've been reading about. Real people, make-believe people, dogs and unicorns, even objects like pencils all feature and these diaries all have one thing in common – they are JAM-PACKED with imagination!

We live and breathe creativity here at Young Writers – it gives us life! We want to pass our love of the written word onto the next generation and what better way to do that than to celebrate their writing by publishing it in a book!

It sets their work free from homework books and notepads and puts it where it deserves to be – OUT IN THE WORLD! Each awesome author in this book should be **super proud** of themselves, and now they've got proof of their imagination, their ideas and their creativity in black and white, to look back on in years to come!

Now that I've read all these diaries, I've somehow got to pick some winners! Oh my gosh it's going to be difficult to choose, but I'm going to have SO MUCH FUN doing it!

Bye!

Jess

Contents

The Diaries

Country Walk

Dear Diary,

I am pretty exhausted now but what an amazing adventure we had! I loved scampering through the leafiness and noticing mini wildlife lurking in the hidden depths of the forest.

During the two-hour journey to the 'Country Walk' estate, I felt cheery when I recognised we were travelling through the route where spring cattle grazed and golden daffodils that stood in bunches perfect for a bouquet.

At first, we proceeded on the rocky pavement with my younger brother leading the way. Soon, we found a peaceful river just beneath an emerald bridge. I asked my dad if we could drink the water and he said yes! So, me and my mum carefully walked on the swirly bark descending towards the edge of the water. As I took a sip of the water, I expected it to be disgusting but it was delicious! Happily, we rambled across the thousand-acre forest filled with nature. Whilst we were trekking, I noticed tiny ladybugs sitting patiently on the soft moss and crunchy leaves. I think some were going through the process of reproduction! After all, it is spring! I have had a phenomenal day!

Akshaya Venkatachalam (12)

The Incredible Diary Of... Derek

An extract

Dear Diary,

The first thing you need to know about me is that my name is Derek. Derek Hardscrabble. I'm eleven years old, in Year 4 and have one day left until the start of the Christmas holidays. I'll leave how I look to your imagination (but please imagine me less like a wimp and more like Batman).

Now, you're probably thinking, 'Why are you eleven and in Year 4?' but this where my story begins... 7:30am, Friday.

After falling over in the shower and forgetting my raincoat, I limped my way to school on the wet, muddy road in the freezing cold sleet. I took a glance at my brand-new Rolex watch and realised that I was half an hour early, for once. As I approached the uninviting silhouette of Winterbourne Primary, I spotted some trees with dry, protective leaves to keep me out of the cold, but unluckily Luke, Simon and Amy were there...

Just in case you didn't know who those names belonged to, Luke and Co. are the school bullies. Luke is the 'leader' - mainly seen with long blonde bangs, a ripped school shirt complete with tatty Nike trainers.

He struts around the school after fighting the teachers, fusses over the #hashtaggirls (social media freaks), and writes rude comments in the boys' loos. Amy usually has flame-red hair pulled back sharply in a spiky punk ponytail (sometimes it is pink), a large, baggy grass-stained shirt and a tiny black skirt that exposes most of her legs. Her face? About as sweet as a *lemon*. Simon has ghastly facial features so revolting that a single look at a swimming pool would dry it up in an instant.

Anyway, I decided to take the chance to face them. Feeling new confidence (or was it just this morning's Snickers), I strode towards them, ready for anything. Suddenly all that confidence evaporated as Luke sneered, "Well, well, well, look who's here chaps!" I retreated as I realised the truth.

"Um, well, I'll just go now because thi... thi... this is probably not the right place to stop." As I cautiously took steps back, I recoiled in horror - Simon was reaching for the scruff of my neck and had picked me up.

"Aargh!" I screamed, thrashing desperately to get out of the bully's grip, "Help me!"

Just then, Amy revealed herself from behind a tree and crooned, "Aww, what a coot, ickle-wickle baby!"...

Marcy Peg Freestone (11)

New Morning

Dear Diary

That morning, it was not the pungent smell of smoke that had awoken me. Not the ear-piercing sound of bullets hitting innocent villagers just feet away. Nor the brutal cold lingering over me. Not the ravenous monster of hunger seeping into my empty stomach. No, not one of these things had woken me up this time. On this occasion, it was the small sound I hadn't heard in what felt like an eternity. It was the peaceful song of birds.

I lay there in silence, listening to its tranquil tune, hoping with my life that song would never end. Begging my mind that this dream would never finish. But it wasn't a dream, was it? Fingers of light reached through the thin curtains, radiating my skin in a blanket of pleasant warmth. With a wave of realisation, it hit me and I remembered. The storm of last night. How far we walked. I knew where I was.

All of a sudden, the sweet aroma of delicious food wafted up my nostrils. Yep, I definitely knew where I was. A smile sprawled across my face. So, eventually, I can finally say this: I am a refugee and I have found home.

Lucy Jones

Draco's Diary

An extract

Dear Diary,

I am writing in this journal today, mostly because it was a birthday present from my mother. I swore to myself that if anyone sees me writing in this thing, then I will hex them and move to a different school! I've never really liked Hogwarts anyway, especially because Potter and his mudblood friend, Granger, is here. Oh yes - Weasley is here too. I was forced to come here by Father, although he never came when he was my age, and unfortunately, my mother agreed.

Things have been peaceful after the defeat of The Dark Lord but that doesn't mean that Potter is acting normal about it. In my opinion, all he had to do was aim a spell at him once that annoying snake, Nagini, was killed (I've never told the Dark Lord that, but I can't now he's gone) and he would have won the 'almighty' battle.

Anyway, let me tell you about what happened today. First, I woke up, quite looking forward to what lessons I had: double potions, defence against the dark arts, transfiguration and flying. Because Crabbe and Goyle had moved school to Durmstrang the previous day, I was on my own.

I made my way to breakfast in the Great Hall whilst muttering different hexes and spells I could use on the helpless first-year Gryffindors (and maybe even Potter) later today. I tried not to make eye contact with any of the professors whilst I was eating (they have never been very friendly towards me once they found out I was a Death Eater, and I wish I hadn't become one now), and then I went to potions.

When I told you my day was going to be good, I was wrong. I was paired with the people I hate for most subjects: Potter for potions, Weasley for defence against the dark arts (he's got better since the battle of Hogwarts), Granger for transfiguration and most unfortunately, Longbottom for flying - he's terrible at it!

The first thing I did after lessons was go to Slytherin common room. I was due to write a letter to my mother but I couldn't be bothered...

Lucy Whitelegge (11)

Apollo 11 Space Log

An extract

Dear Diary,

We have taken off. Yay. *Not.* After seven years, (yeah, seven!) spent training with two astronauts, Neil and Buzz, arguing about who steps on the moon first, I had almost convinced the others that I would do it. Then Mission Control came in and ruined *everything* by putting *me* in last place, Neil first and Buzz second. (I mean, really? Buzz! What kind of a name is that?)

We have been flying for seven minutes and I am seriously considering jumping off the spacecraft and hoping I land on Earth, despite the dangers...

I can see continents now, we have been flying for fifteen minutes and it's beautiful. *Woah!* I have to hold my log down because anti-gravity is taking its toll. But I am drifting off. I guess this concludes my entry for today. Bye! Or could it be tonight? I don't know, time-telling is difficult when all you can see is black!

Dear Diary,

You know, it took me a while to figure out how to write in space. But I did, so hooray! I think. Any young people reading should stop because I don't want to give them bad ideas about being angry with fellow astronauts.

At least I *can* stand on the moon, unlike so many people. Well what do you know, I feel quite superior! The moon's getting closer and Buzz swears he saw an alien. But no one believes him. At least *I* don't! Neil, however, has just been a pain in the neck. He's been trying to think of something cool to say on the moon. The worst one, his favourite, is, "One small step for man, one giant leap for mankind." I know! How cheesy can you get?

Anyway, how come Buzz and I don't get a catchphrase? Just because Mission Control have favouritism doesn't mean me and Buzz are left in the dumps, shadowing his fame...

Sophie Amelia Smith (9)

The Incredible Diary Of...

6th March 2019

Dear Diary,

I have been dying to tell you this extraordinary piece of news. It all happened at school today and it calls for a celebration! That's how amazing it is! Unable to prevent myself from quaking, I sat nervously on my sapphire chair; I could sense the tension in the drab room. Honestly, it was really surprising to think that the atmosphere in a room could change from a jubilant, amiable area to an anxious, nonplussed space within seconds.

"Charlotte!" my teacher, Mrs Cookley, called exuberantly from outside the gloomy, dreary classroom. "You're first!"

Charlotte went out, looking pale. Desperately, I hoped she would be alright. The rest of the class listened intently to the voices of Mrs Cookley and Charlotte.

Ten minutes later, Charlotte came in, grinning from ear to ear. Sweat broke out and colour flooded my face; I knew she did well, but I was soon compelled to be tense.

After four more children went to have a personal chat, my hands were quivering like mad because it was my turn next. But little did I know that I was in for a magnificent moment.

When Mrs Cookley called me, which seemed to take an eternity, I stood up and walked out of the room.

Immediately, I could feel the atmosphere change. It was a colourful corridor with banners on display that read: 'Congratulations'. Harmonious music was heard by my sharp ears and I felt my spirits rise considerably.

"Well done!" my teacher beamed. "You got full marks in every test! That is the highest in the year group!"

I stood rooted to the spot, stunned. Could it be? For the first time, I felt joyous! I entered the class, as proud as a peacock.

It's dinner time. Mum made a treat.

See you later,

Twarita

Twarita Gundi (11)

The Incredible Diary Of... Henry!

An extract

Dear Diary,

Today hasn't been great, but it hasn't been bad either.

The wind rushed in my face, causing my eyes to water. I loved to fly, my speckled wings outspread like an angel. Flying meant freedom, freedom meant... well, I don't know what but it brings me a bundle of happiness like an everlasting pile of greasy chips all for me!

I glanced at the cloudy grey sky and immediately swerved to avoid a collision with a plane. After that, I remembered I needed to keep my eyes below but when I did, I was greeted by ocean as far as the eye could see. The waves were like great walls of grey-green as they dashed over a nearing island, gleaming spray flew from them, white in the stormy sky.

When I eventually reached the land, the weather was miraculously and impossibly completely different. I let the morning sun wash over me as I bathed in the delicious warmth of the fast-rising sun. I soared over rosy-red gates with the engraved markings: *Sir Billy's Fairground.*

A dozen seagulls greeted me as I perched on top of a run down carousel. Out of the corner of my eye, I saw an overweight man swing a golden key out of his pocket to the gate. This didn't bother me but in his right hand, fat, greasy chips drizzled with squiggles of tomato sauce, wrapped in yesterday's newspaper. The other seagulls hadn't noticed! I took my chance and zoomed off the plastic horse and hurled a chip off the pile. The man glared at me, his face as red as an angry sunset. He threw a pebble at me, knocking my balance, so I give him back a little present from above.

Let's just say he'll regret his Olympic throw once he realises the slop strewn down on his bald head...

Tamsyn Sayles (10)

The Terrifying Captain Cocktail
An extract

Tuesday, 8th February 2019

Dear Diary,

Today I was in the library, looking for a book about dinosaurs when I needed the toilet. I went upstairs, as usual, I shut the door and sat down.

Two minutes later, I opened the door and walked out into a now dark library! I walked down the spiralling staircase to the ground floor, looking for Kathrine and Liam, the librarians. But terror-struck, I noticed that it was dark down here too and no one was about. I walked to the main door and pulled but it didn't open! I looked around for my book but it had been tidied away and a different book was in its place: 'Captain Cocktail's Diary'. The room was suddenly filled with a strange purple light and even stranger, I heard waves crashing and the creak of rigging in the wind. I seemed to be pulled towards the old, dusty book. It opened itself up to a diary entry: The 8th of February, 1641. The book glowed brighter than ever! I felt my body disappear beneath me, and zoomed so fast into the book that I fainted.

When I woke up I heard a noise of ringing bells. I stood up shakily and found myself on a dock in a pair of ragged shorts and a red and white, rum-stained T-shirt. Next to me was a man in some black, ripped trousers and a belt which held a pistol. He had an eye patch and a scarlet, brown-buttoned jacket which swept down to just below his thighs. His hair had several hair toggles dangling on his many plaits. He had dark eyes under bushy eyebrows. Bullets hung on a string from his jacket pocket. Two more guns poked out either side of his trousers.

He was staring towards a docked ship which had three masts bearing sails emblazoned with a skull and crossbones...

Harry Stockton (9)

The Incredible Diary Of... Goldilocks!

An extract

Dear Diary,

I've been meaning to share a lot with someone but I haven't found the right person. Then, Baby Bear suggested that I could mark down all my opinions and thoughts in a diary. To tell you the truth, that bear's brain is way greater than his body! Truly, he thinks of things that I'd never fathom, things that wouldn't reach the furthest corners of my wildest imagination! So here I am, writing everything that is unfair in my life!

First of all, I would like to tell you that you can't believe everything in a fairy tale. The fact that my life is *based* on a fairy tale is so humiliating! I have to do whatever is engraved and printed in a scrappy book! It should be the life of my author, not mine!

Anyhow, nothing will change by me sulking and nit-picking over it. The fact is that everything that has happened and will happen will be at Robert Southey's will (the man who wrote the story on which I have to live my days). Actually, if things went *my* way, I would never eat porridge! Yes, I, Goldilocks, hate porridge.

Did you ever believe that you'd hear me, Goldilocks, say something like that? Well I think the answer is no. The way it melts in your mouth and covers your throat is way too appalling for me.
I am not meant to be telling you all this but if you are reading this right now, that means you have found my diary and at long last, I can divulge all my secrets. Furthermore, in the book, it says that my hair is pure blonde and silky. Actually, my hair isn't that bright at all. It actually has brown highlights. If they wanted to feature me in a book, they could at least describe me correctly...

Aanya Gupta (11)

Ocean Eyes

An extract

14th April
Dear Diary,
Today I collected coconuts from the new harvest trees. I've just taught Carlo how to climb the bark. As he's only eight, I think he did quite well. I tried to teach him as well as the orangutans taught me. I walked along the beach and chose some shells for my collection too. For supper, I cooked mealworms with some cod. Yummy! I wish Mum and Dad could see how far Carlo and I have come. They'd have been so proud. I know they would.
Maria.

30th May
Dear Diary,
Carlo has just learnt to sail! Right now, he is sailing around the island. Milo has just had twins! If you don't know who Milo is, he is my pet turtle. I adopted him when we first came. It's Carlo's ninth birthday very soon and I have a huge surprise planned.
Maria.

8th June

Dear Diary,

It's Carlo's birthday! When I told him the big surprise, he was over the moon. So, in twelve days, we will sail to a bigger island which is more exciting. It's about 300 miles away and there are Greek myths about it (Dad told me that). I know you think I'm crazy but I owe it to myself and I owe it to Carlo. Nearly all of our lives we've lived on this tiny island and we haven't seen a town or any shops or anything like that in eight years. Just sand, sea, palm trees and fruit.

Maria.

19th June

Dear Diary,

Don't tell Carlo this but I'm a bit nervous about tomorrow. When Mum and Dad left for the afternoon that day, they said they would be back by sunset. That evening, there was a huge storm and angry rain as hard as stones and howling wind as loud as wolves...

Eliza Lucy Robson Brown (10)

The Unexpected Goblin Invasion

An extract

Dear Diary,

Yes! Victory and freedom! It's Friday! Everybody knows Friday evenings are amazingly thrilling! Since I finally came back from school, I decided to watch many very epic episodes of some sort, on TV... As I was right in the middle of an episode, I heard a loud crash, it was probably as loud as fifteen fireworks booming at the same time!

What on Earth was that sound? I thought. I dashed to the window, sprinting as fast as I could ever run! I was freaked out. My heart was pounding, I slowly and carefully pulled a teensy weensy, tiny bit of the curtain to the side and peeked outside and you'll never actually believe this! Okay, there was a goblin getting his hoverboard off the ground. He didn't look brutal but he *did* look like he was up to something and I thought the goblin was just in my head! But in no time, he was floating on his hoverboard. Honestly, I'd love to be on one of those. I ran into my colossal backyard.

"Hey! What are you doing here?" I shouted.

"Ha, ha, ha!" laughed the goblin.

His laugh made me a nervous wreck.

"I am gonna conquer the human dimension and I don't care whether you're fine with that idea or not!"

I ran, jumped and managed to land on the goblin's extreme hoverboard.

"Get off my hover... thingy, whatever it's called, and let me finish my plan in peace!" The goblin actually sounded quite grim, then he pushed me off. There was a humongous splash and then I fell in my swimming pool and, I woke up.

"It was a *dream?* Aargh!"

It was Friday morning, so I had to go to school...

Vasuman Gupta (9)

The Girl Who Hoped

An extract

Monday, 18th March

Dear Diary,

I always stand out in a crowd. I can't do half the things my friends can do. I was born with a disability. I have to be in a wheelchair all the time. My name is Amanda Small. I am thirteen years old. I've always hated climate change, just like Greta Thunberg. She's amazing! She stands in front of lots of important people who are in charge of large countries and tells them how bad climate change is and that we should do something about it before we run out of time. Greta really inspires me because she does exactly what I've always wanted to do, make everybody stop and think about what they're doing to the world! All my friends are going to the climate change march and I've just got to go with them. Mum won't let me because I'm stuck in the wheelchair! It's not fair, just not fair!

Tuesday, 19th March

Dear Diary,

Just great. All of my friends are going to the march and I'm not. I wish Mum would let me go. It would be so fun!

22

Mum says it would be too difficult as I am in a wheelchair and to get me up to London would be too hard. To tell you the truth, I am inclined to go on my own. Maybe I will! The march is this Friday and *everyone* is talking about it - even teachers! Basically, everyone except me, of course. What if they met Greta without me! That would be so unfair! I've sent letters to Greta, she *has* written back but meeting her in person, wow! It would be a dream come true! If my friends met her and I wasn't there, it would be a nightmare come true! I could go crazy just thinking about it...

Clea Huddleston (10)

The Incredible Diary Of... My Talking Pets

Dear Diary,

I know that this might seem a little crazy and hard to believe but I can talk to my pets. It's amazing. I can understand my pets' feelings and everything! Sometimes normal humans that can't speak to pets find it hard to see what their pets need or want. I have four horses, two ponies and two dogs. The names of my four horses are Spirit, Chicalinda, Boomerang (he's the hungry one) and Coco. The names of my ponies are Milly and Molly. Last but not least, my dogs. Their names are Ruby and Rascal.

On my tenth birthday, I received two Arabian mares, especially from Turkey. They came with Turkish names, Aktogali and Alee. They were amazingly super-duper fast!

A month ago, my dog, Ruby, had broken her paw and was lost. I saw she had not come home in a couple of days.

The next day, I was determined to find her. I saddled up Aktogali and spoke to my animals and told them to help look for her. All the animals and I went to look for her. Until... Alee shouted, "Footprints! Fur!"

We gasped as I burst into tears. Milly, Molly and Rascal were amazing at sniffing things, especially food.

Two hours later, I got off my horse and noticed something in the distance. Aktogali had great hearing as well as Spirit, Chicalinda and Boomerang. Also, Coco could not come, she was unwell.

"Ruby!" I shouted.

She barked weakly. We raced towards her, I lifted her up and took her back.

Two weeks later, she was ready again. Aktogali, Alee and Ruby all ran together.

The next day, we had a long chat with all the animals. I sat on Alee and the animals and I ran like a herd.

Zayna Mushtaq

The Incredible Diary Of... A Bully

An extract

9th January 2019.

Dear Diary,

This is not just a diary. Just because I wrote 'Diary' doesn't mean I *meant* diary. This is *clearly* a journal! Be warned!

Anyway, my name is Brandon Wills and I am not your mate. I am a bully.

So, today wasn't the most pleasant of all days. It was Mother's Day so most of the nice female teachers were at home, except Mrs Lozano and Mrs Haiyan who had grown-up children that were already living on their own. Worst of all, we had maths today and Mr Sadoon was our substitute teacher. Let me give a brief description of him. He was the strict Lithuanian teacher with an American accent just like everyone else.

Maths was the first lesson today, so I had to deal with an angry man shouting cube numbers in my face. We had break after maths since it was a half-day. I wedgied a bunch of vulnerable nerds on the playground. But one nerd got lucky and had some hot sauce in his lunch box. He earned himself a first-class ticket to detention town and a punch in the face!

In English class, I was devastated, absolutely devastated. Mrs Lozano sent me and Nevel (the hot sauce nerd) out of the classroom because she was so disappointed, and I got sent to the Deputy Head for my own punishment. Any normal person would think I got shouted at but worse still, I got suspended and my parents gave me a horrible surprise. Don't ask me what it was!

10th January 2019
Dear Diary,
I am going for a one-day Bully Learning Programme. Here I am, and it is break time. This place is really like a school for bullies and you can hardly walk through the hallway without being wedgied...

David Olanrewaju Olugbaro (10)

The Incredible Diary Of... Mr Box

An extract

Dear Diary,

Today I learnt that I was moving house because my owner, Dillan Wilson, moved to a new school because he got bullied in the other one. And because I've been a good pet and I've been making my owner laugh and all that, I get... wait for it... a whole new room to myself! It has the best stuff and toys as well, like the £50 massage bean bag and back-itching robot. It's a robot that itches your back and it cost £599! My owner also got a big room for me because I'm a very big box and maybe a little bit overweight. And because I've got a lot of stuff inside me like: batteries, paper, old photographs of me and my owner's family, spare pieces of old cars, cards, rubbish and, basically nothing else really.

Fun fact: boxes get bigger by putting stuff inside them. For example, if I put a ruler inside me, I would grow thirty centimetres longer. But obviously, we boxes need to lose weight because if we gain too much weight, we will explode into smithereens. And to lose weight, we have to stop eating for a very long time which is very hard if you ask me.

Five months after I was born, me and my mum were under attack by the boxes of Royal Mail. They are vicious boxes that are used by wretched and horrific hunters that want to kill every jungle box to make box stew and sell them to make more money. So my mum put me inside her so that the boxes of Royal Mail can't find me and she ran to save herself from the terrible nightmare.
A few days later I got bored inside her so I asked if I could get out but the answer was obvious, she was going to say no...

Ahmet Kamil Culhaoglu (10)

Nearly Rumbled!

An extract

Dear Diary,

All is going well this summer. I am so excited to tell you about a very peculiar day on Granny's farm! I woke up and it was another sunny day on Granny's Irish farm. We were spending the summer holidays with Granny whilst our mum and dad went to Scotland for a work conference.

I jumped out of bed and woke Tiarnan and Lorcan up. We stumbled down the stairs to the sight of three neatly laid plates with delicious toast with creamy butter on. Once we'd finished, we asked Granny if we could go and play outside. She told us we could go, but only if we fed the pigs and were back inside by five o'clock for dinner.

As we heaved the heavy bucket of last night's leftovers to the pigs, the stench burned our noses. The pigs scoffed the food greedily and then snorted with delight.

At last, we ran free to the hills to play in the mucky vast range of green grass. The wind rushed past our cheeks like knives and left a rosy pink colour in our cheeks. Ruby the dog's ears flapped around in the wind.

We were playing a game of 'tip team' when Lorcan noticed that Ruby wasn't with us anymore. We ran past the cows, pigs, sheep and chickens in search of Ruby, but it was no use. We just couldn't find her.

After a moment I took a quick glance over to the wall separating Granny's house from Moody Margory's house (Granny's neighbour). I saw Ruby's tail wag momentarily before it disappeared through a gap in the wall. We tried to squeeze through it one at a time and eventually, we all made it through and then the chase began...

Naoise McManus (10)

The Diary Of Goldilocks

An extract

Dear Diary,

You can't believe the day I just had. It was terrible! While walking down the street I was feeling famished and wanted something to eat. Then I saw a small cottage just the height of a Medlar tree. Since it was extremely tiny I thought that it was abandoned so I went inside. To my delight, I couldn't believe there were three porridges (oats and syrup). As you know, I was hungry and ate the first porridge. It was too hot! My tongue was on fire. Still hungry, I decided to eat the second porridge. It was awfully cold!

Finally, since I was longing for food, I tried the third bowl and to my pleasure, it was delightful and I wanted to have more. It was not too hot or cold but just right.

After that pleasant meal, I was quite exhausted and wanted to sit down. Then I saw three chairs. Of course, I was going to sit. The first chair was too high and my short self couldn't reach it.

Afterwards, I really wanted to sit down so I sat down on the second chair. OMG! I couldn't believe it. Nothing was my size. The chair was extremely huge. What creature could fit in *that* chair?

Lastly, I was pleading to God that this chair was just right for me. Then as if it was a miracle, the chair was *my size!* So jubilantly, I started to bounce up and down on the chair. Suddenly it broke! I mean, really? Am I that heavy? I don't even weigh more than a stone.

This was an accident. I didn't mean to break the chair and anyway, this house is abandoned.

By this time, I was tremendously dog-tired and actually needed to sleep...

Avril Nakibirango Luyindi (11)

The Incredible Diary Of...

An extract

Dear Diary,

Today has been the best school day of my life. It has been so interesting and enjoyable as we went to the space museum!

When we arrived at school, we were allowed to pick who we sat next to on the coach. I went with my best friend, Lily. We played many games on the way there, like rock, paper, scissors, I spy, add on and who can spot a motorbike first. I won all of these games apart from rock, paper, scissors. When we arrived, we were allowed to go and look around the museum with our partners. Lily and I saw many different astronaut suits, model rockets and model planets. As well as looking at space models and astronaut suits, we had to read some facts about the planets in our solar system and the ones we liked the most, we would have to write down on an A4 piece of lined paper that our teacher gave us. The reason why we had to do this was because we had to do a space poster on all the planets when we got back to school so the teacher could select the best ones to put on display.

My favourite facts about each planet were: Mercury is the smallest planet in our solar system, Venus is the hottest planet, Earth is the only planet that scientists know has life on, Mars is around 227,940,000km from the sun, Jupiter has sixty-seven known moons, Saturn is best known for the bright, beautiful rings that circle its equator. The rings are made up of countless particles of ice and rock that each orbit Saturn independently. Uranus was officially discovered by Sir William Herschel in 1781 and Neptune takes 165 Earth years to orbit the sun...

Summer Meek (11)

Away In The Rainforest

Dear Diary.

Today was an amazing day! As I'm an explorer, I discover different types of species so us humans get to know about them. Yesterday, I was given my first job of being an explorer. I had to go to this rainforest to look up a creature. But the expedition turned out as a disaster.

It began when I was walking with my other companions through the rainforest where there's a variety of animals. It was amazing! There were parrots everywhere and there were so many fish in the river. I warned

my friends that there could be a lot of over-protective species here and they should be cautious. I gave them a lighter so they could create smoke and then we'll know where they are. I *knew* this was a bad idea.

I saw mesmerising animals filling the whole forest, it was lovely. Suddenly, I saw the smoke. One of my friends was in danger!

When I got there, I saw that one of my friends had been bitten by an animal

which I then found out was thought to be extinct, Hunginades. I found out there was a medicinal plant to cure my friend's cut called 'splodge-aid'.

The bad news was it was surrounded by aggressive grumplehags. We discovered what they love the most was lemons (they had a unique taste). So we found a few lemons and threw one to the opposite direction of the splodge-aid. The grumplehags followed it excitedly.

Finally, we got drops of it and gave it to my friend. He was cured!

Later in London, we showed our boss our findings. Then the amazed man gave us an award for bravery. I couldn't believe it. I was so happy.

Tevin Kailainathan

The Incredible Diary Of...

An extract

Dear Diary,

As I write this journal, I think back to the time where I passed the day playing football with my friends. Then everything changed. My life turned upside down. The war broke out. All the boys who were the perfect age to go in the army had to sign up to fight for the country and if they didn't, they would look like cowards. Since I was a year younger, I couldn't join but my older brother did. A few weeks later, a telegraph came saying that my brother was in hospital and was in a serious condition. I prayed hard but my prayer was unanswered. My brother died the next morning. To avenge my brother's death, I lied about my age and I signed up when they came on the next round looking for more people for the army. Nobody suspected that I was a year younger because I was tall for my age.

Today was my first day. We had to sneak into a place called no man's land. Many of us were caught trying to sneak in and were taken as prisoners. I was nearly caught but I managed to run and hide behind the tanks.

At that moment, I had touched my face and I felt sweat breaking through it. I could hear officers from no-man's-land. *Hurry up!* I screamed silently in my head. I licked my lips, they tasted salty and gritty. Being careful of the underground bombs, I quickly ran across the land and threw the bomb that I was supposed to throw into no-man's-land. Behind me, I could hear the underground bombs setting off and killing my fellow officers. After disposing of the bomb, I turned and ran back to my homeland...

Jahanavee Sandeep (10)

The Time Of Rome

An extract

Dear Diary,

In a little Scottish village called Carluke, something no one could explain happened. Time travel, yes, time travel was discovered by me! My name is Olivia but you can call me Lilly. I'm fourteen years old and I love chocolate!

I was walking home, as usual, and when I got home, I saw something I had never seen before. There was a spiky hole in the wall so I pulled it to see what happened. To my surprise, it opened like an old crooked door. It squeaked a loud squeak when I opened it and behind the door were some old dusty stairs! Feeling curious and a little bit frightened, I crept down the dusty stairs.

When I got to the bottom of the stairs, a light suddenly switched on. In front of me, I saw a pale blue sheet covering a weird-shaped object. Feeling nervous, I stepped out of my shadow to uncover the mysterious object under the blue sheet. Standing in front of me was a big blue metal box with red buttons, green cables, a colourful screen and some silky red curtains.

Not knowing what it was, I stepped into the box through the silky red curtains. Inside the box was a twirly-whirly chair like the ones you get in photo booths. In front of the chair was a big screen with lots of buttons.

I excitedly sat on the twirly-whirly chair and pressed one of the small red buttons and the chair whizzed round as fast as lightning! I thought myself, *I wonder what that big green button does*, so I pressed it. As I pressed the button, the box started to shake and wobble about. It felt like taking off in an aeroplane...

Rosie Mawson (9)

The Incredible Diary Of... Hemexian

An extract

Dear Diary,

I had a most unusual day today and I simply must tell you about it. You know how I long to visit all those famous and distant places? Well, today, I got my heart's desire. As soon as I woke up, I knew things were different. Instead of my soft net canopy, I looked up at the bright blue April sky and my bed felt extra fluffy. Imagine my surprise when I discovered I was on a cloud, high up in the sky with the birds flying past, bright sunlight all around me and Mrs Brown for company! You know her, don't you? My partner in crime, my dear poodle?

As I was taking this all in, Mrs Brown, as sweet as sugar, asked me if I wanted to visit the Eiffel Tower! Imagine, her talking! And of course, I did! Off we zoomed to France.

The impressive engineering marvel could be seen from far away. Parisians, milled about, enjoying the gorgeous weather. This was supposed to be a whistle-stop tour, but I managed to bribe Mrs Brown with promises of juicy meat chunks under the table and she reluctantly agreed to short stops on the way.

The view from the cloud was spectacular. I peeped in on the diners in the restaurant at the top before Mrs Brown whizzed me off to our next stop - The Taj Mahal.

Over mountains, deserts, green lands and rivers we flew. It was getting warmer and brighter as we drew nearer the tropics. When I looked down from my seat in the clouds, I could see millions of people, who looked like ants, going about their daily lives and the majestic Taj Mahal gleaming white in the sunlight. Oh, what a tribute to love!

Hema Ahuja

The Exciting Picnic Adventure

An extract

Saturday, 13th October 2018

Dear Diary,

Today was the best day ever! It all started when I got a phone call from my best friend, Andrea, asking if we could have a picnic together in the meadow for lunch. I was super excited so I asked my mum and guess what? She said yes!

We started packing the food and decided that Andrea and her mum would bring the main lunch while me and my mum would bring the desserts, drinks and cutlery.

When we got there, Andrea and I wanted to race each other in the field while the mums got everything set out. We were just about to start when Andrea's mum called her to help set out everything. I was just about to go and help as well when I heard a noise coming from a mushroom. It sounded like a magical, twinkling sound. I was pretty sure I was imagining it but as I walked closer to it, the sound became louder and louder until finally, I was standing right next to it.

After thinking about it for a good five minutes, I lifted up the top of the mushroom and saw, to my delight, a tiny, small world with fairies and elves inside! Slowly, I touched the pink glitter surrounding the top of the mushroom and, to my surprise, I shrank to the size of the fairies and elves! I didn't know what to do so I walked around and followed a few fairies around. It was all peaceful and beautiful in the new wonderland.
"Hello, you don't look like a fairy or an elf," said a soft voice, "are you lost?"
I turned around and saw a fairy flying in mid-air. I was startled but amazed at the same time...

Aanya Dhanani (10)

The Incredible Diary Of... Om Nom

An extract

Dear Diary,

Today, the most unspeakable thing happened to me! I was guarding my owner's belongings when I heard a crackle strangely like that of a firework.

"Is she gone?" whispered a tinkly voice as a young unicorn's face looked down at me.

"Yep. She's probably at school by now," I replied to this exquisite creature; it was my friend, Snowy.

"About time! I thought she was never going to leave!" complained her older sister, Crystal, as she wriggled out of her position in the basket to stretch herself and shake away the aching cramps which plagued her body like an unwanted cold.

A loud purr reverberated around the room as all eyes in the room swivelled round to see who had made this loud, comforting noise. *Thwack!* A lurid smack froze all the movements and sounds in the room.

"It's okay, guys! I accidentally slapped the pillow trying to turn around. I'm big, you know!" Dip called out, instantly slicing through the silence.

I relaxed my mouth as I had clamped it shut in a desperate attempt to keep her treasures safe.

Soon the area transformed into a hive of excitement as all my roommates bustled about their own business.

Daisy asked if anybody wanted any breakfast and boy! You would've never seen so many shouts start up so quickly before! Even *I* was hungry. So, she set to work on the small kitchen set in the corner and soon, everyone had a scrumptious breakfast set before them! She even gave me my favourite snack - peppermint sweets! Yum!

Fatima Imran (10)

The Diary Of A Suffragette

Dear Diary,

Today has been the most frightfully awful day of my life. I am now sitting and writing this entry after writing to Ma and the rest of the family back in Birmingham. Many are saying that the sun won't set until midnight again, so I am dreading yet another restless night. It has been so swelteringly hot for almost a week and I have had no time to write my diary as both little nine-year-old Betty and Charles are seriously ill (as bad as I've ever seen them) and in hospital. Ma has been so busy with the suffragettes and Pa with work that it is now my responsibility to visit my poor siblings in hospital and leave my suffragette post to Ma. Only last month, poor darling Mary (who has never so much as hurt a fly) was arrested, for reasons not even the policeman who arrested her knew, but all the same was locked up, for God knows how long! And only yesterday, according to Ma, both Jane and Elizabeth were locked up for the same unknown reasons. Although more and more people are getting put behind bars, gossip has it, that the public is debating even more about our cause and that maybe, by next year, we might even win the vote!

I must hurry as I have just checked the time and Big Ben has just chimed eight o'clock which means it has been two hours since I last visited Betty and Charles and should visit them again. I do hope I do not catch this awful illness that is spreading or else I may have to postpone my 21st birthday celebrations next week, to next month instead. Barbara

Asha Kirkpatrick (11)

The Incredible Diary Of... The New Girl

An extract

Sunday, 31st August

Dear Diary,

Moved to a new town, started a new school, left all my mates behind... Yes, this normally might be a nightmare but I wasn't terrified. In fact, I was pretty much delighted with the whole thing. Mainly because I am finally out of the horribly unfair control of my so-called friend, Lydia, which pretty much means I was her servant. Now everything's going to change. I'm going to get a fresh, new start where nobody knows anything about me and I'm going to make myself 'the (popular) new girl'. I put 'popular' in brackets because I don't particularly like the fame and I prefer to make myself invisible. But anyway, new girls are expected to be popular, in my opinion.

Monday, 1st September

Dear Diary,

Oh no! This has not turned out too well. I didn't even have the proper school uniform. Eeek! I knew I was going to be the odd one out!

I tried to match the uniform. Ugh! Sooo unsuccessful, I couldn't even find a tie. Anyway, I hate ties that make me look like a businessman, so I ended up
wearing a pink T-shirt and black skirt. But that was not the worst of my day.
The worst was, I sobbed in maths class 'cause I got told off for not finishing
my work on time... So ashamed! How embarrassing!
The friend thingy wasn't too bad. Wendy, one of the PPPs (popular, proud and pretty) came in asking to be my bestie and gave me a welcome present, sweet!
She helped me sort through everything, easy-peasy!

Meng Tong Yin (11)

The Incredible Diary Of... JoJo Siwa

Dear Diary,

I woke up in the morning and it was 7am so I got out of bed and went to brush my teeth.

After, I had a warm shower. I went into my big, pretty room and put on a pink top with blue jeans, a pink shiny jacket and a pink rainbow bow. I went down for breakfast and my mum was getting it ready. I had toast, eggs and beans. Then I went into my room and got ready for school. My mum drove me there and dropped me at the black gate. Then I saw my two best friends near the girls' lockers. We laughed as we ran into class.

In class, we had to make a 3D road stop in the USA. I thought it was going to be tricky but in the end, mine looked brilliant and was the best out of the whole class. Finally, it was lunchtime because I was starving. I had roast dinner with chicken and gravy. For pudding, I had a cupcake with chocolate on top.

A few hours later, it was home time and my friends and I had a great day. Our friend asked us if we wanted to go to her house and we said yes! We called our mums and they said yes too so we got there, went in and locked the front door.

We went upstairs and saw Lily's room. First we did our nails and we got to do another JoJo video. It was an experiment for candy!
A few minutes later, Lily's mum called us for dinner. We all had fish and chips for dinner and apple pie for pudding. We all went home and I was all ready for bed.
"I hope I have another day like this!" I said and went to bed.

Naima Regha (9)

The Incredible Diary Of... The Bird

Dear Diary,

I was a normal, ordinary bird until it happened, the crash. I was startled at first but I still went forward to look. It was amazing. It was like a big rock but I could see something trying to break free. I flew closer until I saw it, an odd-looking creature had come out. It looked around until it saw me, it looked like a bird (like me) but a greenish-blueish colour, but I didn't think it was even from Earth! I knew that I had to hide it from the so-called humans and that agency that studies strange, odd people and I hear the treatment there is terrible so I took the strange space bird to my cave. I then found out he can fly. I named him GB because he is kind of green and blue.

When I would fly out to get some food for us, he would always be sunbathing just outside the cave. Then the weather started to get worse and it started snowing and snowing so we had to stay in but as I was sleeping, he snuck off.

I quickly woke up to find out what had happened so I quickly went to search for him.

I found him in a horrible place, the FBI building. They had found him! My worst nightmare! I knew I had to help him get out and back up to space so I snuck in and I did it before they could do any tests on him.

He was safe and something very weird happened - he started floating all the way to space and I shouted goodbye. It was the happiest moment of my life and that's why I wrote this diary entry, so the world could know about this.

Ayomide Deborah Aboyeji (10)

The Incredible Diary Of... Sweetie

Dear Diary,

My name is Sweetie the sweet. Today I had my favourite breakfast of marshmallow cereal, which made me happy.

Next, I put on my uniform. When I am at school, I wear a blue top that has a cute cat on it. In addition to this, I wear a pair of stripy trousers, which are as stripy as a zebra. Have you ever worn anything as fabulous as me?

I go on the candy bus every day to arrive at school on time. The amazing bus has lollipops painted all over it. On the bus every day, there is a pink trolley, where there are toys; you can get one toy for every journey you take. Today, I set my eyes upon a cute bunny. I then got it from the glistening trolley. But then I saw the ultra-rare unicorn. I wanted the unicorn, so I did a trade.

"We are here," said Mr Fun, the bus driver.

"Today we are going to learn how to make toys," announced Miss Party, my teacher.

"Wow!" I said.

Then we started making toys. It was really fun. I think my favourite part was making the ears.

When it was break time, I went on the climbing frame. As I went down the slide, I saw a new see-saw. I went to try it out with my friend who was very excited. On one end of the see-saw was a cake for my friend to sit on and a gummy bear for me. When the bell rang, it meant that it was time to go back to class. In class, we learnt about food. At lunch, all of us ate burgers. I think they are the best burgers in the world.
That was what I did today.

Maha Gnanachandran (7)

The Incredible Diary Of... My Pencil

An extract

Dear Diary,

Being alone in a dark, horrible leather rag which humans call a pencil case is not fun. I hate being a pencil, it is the worst thing in the world. *Zip!* Huh? What was that? What's happening? Why am I being picked up? Wait a minute, I'm being put down again, phew. Hang on, why is biro being picked up? This can only mean one thing. Joshua's got his pen licence. I'm never going to be used again, apart from being chewed! Oh no, pencils are not meant to be chewed. Here it comes... I'm being picked up and into the mouth I go.

"Joshua," a loud voice says, "you're not allowed to use a pen yet, you don't have your licence."

Biro was put down and I was writing, yay! I've got another week till Josh gets his licence.

It's break time now and Josh is taking me out with him. Thank goodness I'm not going to be in that pencil case again. Josh is talking to his friends at the moment, probably talking about how cool his pencil is.

"I hate my pencil!" shouts Josh to his friends. "I want to use my biro, it cost £8."

You know how I was saying that being in a pencil case is the worst thing in the world? Well the only thing worse is a PE lesson. You have to sit on the desk and watch the children have lots of fun. Josh is on the apparatus and is walking to the edge. Whoa, Josh just did a backflip off the side of it.

Joshua David Samuel Rowe

At The Music Hall

Dear Diary,

This morning it was my birthday! My family had organised a very special surprise. I could not wait to see it!

When we arrived, there was a huge building in front of me! Inside was a stage, chairs and tables. We took a seat and ordered burgers. Suddenly, the ruby-red, mesmerising curtains blew open! The show was starting!

The host announced, "Here are the fabulous, inspiring musicians!"

The audience clapped, the music hall was as loud as a family of bulls running around your house! The first magic trick included an assistant. I raised my hand and went up on stage. The magician said, "I have one ball, can you now tap the ball and blow on it?"

Then two balls appeared! The magician and I both took a bow. I went down to my seat while the introducer announced, "Here are the hilarious comedians!"

Sadly, a comedian was sick so a person who used to be a comedian came up on stage. I was so proud of him, he must have had a lot of courage!

One comedian was telling jokes to another comedian and another comedian was putting up the hood of the comedian who was telling a joke. The comedian who was telling the joke threw his coat and the comedian was so mad that his face turned as red as a fresh tomato!

After that performance, it was time to go!

At home, I told my family that this was my best birthday ever!

Gabriel Desaedeleer (8)

The Incredible Diary Of...

Dear Diary,

I found the creature in our attic on Tuesday evening. It was the day after we had started unpacking. The winter was coming. It was only me. Nobody else. I moved as slowly as I could. It was lying there surrounded in wet (fake) blood. I saw it, it was real at first, then I found out the truth. It was a young lady who was also half-wolf. On a box of food surrounded by blood, she was dusty, covered in dead bluebottles and spiders, with hair as black as the clear night sky. It looked like her dress was dipped in blood, but why would she be here? Out of all places she could be right now, she chose a desolate, almost empty abandoned attic. I thought I saw her blink at me... I took my torch and shone it in. There were hundreds of woodlice scattering away, dusty windows and also broken floorboards and other things. Once I saw it, I ran and rotated away from her. I heard something... I froze and looked down. I stepped on something then I heard faint calls, Mum and Dad were fortunately back.

I cautiously edged past the bones of the creature, with my heart thudding. Breathing heavily, I ran straight to my parents. No turning back. Thrusting the torch away, I screamed at the top of my lungs.

My mum woke me up. It was just a nightmare.
Next, I drank some water and had a good dream.

Samirabonu Ravshanbekova (11)

The Incredible Diary Of... Piper McLean

Dear Diary,

Today was a terrible day, I knew fear, but this was different. I watched as the giant thundered up the ruins and into the room, where Annabeth and I were standing, shaking like two mice being hunted down by a cat.

"Come out, come out wherever you are!" fumed Deimos. "I know you're in here somewhere!"

"We need a plan!" I whispered. "Something that will keep him away from us until we find a way out!"

Unluckily for me, Annabeth stared like I was some sort of three-headed monster.

"That does not seem like a good idea," she whispered, "although, we could use our emergency string to make a net and capture Deimos. But that still sounds kind of risky!"

I glared at her with my best 'death-squint', so she finally gave in and started weaving.

"Just one bit... Done!"

I started acting quickly, we still had to capture Deimos in it and throw him off the cliff.

"I'll lasso the net onto him!" I whispered just loudly enough for Annabeth to hear.

I took the net and with an almighty swing, I threw it onto the bemused giant.

Uljana Dikteriovaite

Blood Is Thicker Than Water, But Justice Is Thicker Than Both

Dear Diary,

I bet you always thought that pens were lifeless, yet my species is just as alive as you. You giants grab us and use our ink as if we're worthless. Though you get your stupid old work done, you probably never even thought that your writing could be murder! Especially not if you throw us into Pen Prison (the bin in your office) when we're out of ink as that is how we die. Like you, we use our blood up. If you useless old creatures waste us, shouldn't we get a chance to waste you?

I woke up to find these minuscule, old figures underneath me. They seemed to be of my kind yet they had sprouted limbs and there were microscopic little strands sticking out of their lids. As I bent down to scoop one up, it gave me a very high-pitched shriek, covered its nib with two arms and curled into an adorable little ball. Looking closely at it, I realised it was a superior giant. Yet it was tiny. I decided to put it down and search for things to do.

Back in my home pencil case, I lay in bed. This must have been some time ago for I was still small.

Then my mother left me to get to sleep yet in a mesmerised state, I had whispered the same thing over and over: "I wish I was a human..."

Tatyana Holdsworth (11)

My Diary About Sasha Corbin

13th July 2019

Dear Diary,

Today was a big day! We were playing Australia in the World Cup. I felt nervous and excited!

I'd just woken up in my hotel room. It was so fancy, my room was huge! It was 6.30am and I was just going to have my breakfast in the restaurant. My sister, Kadeen, was going to meet me there. I had fruit salad, orange juice and eggs on toast. My sister had fruit salad and jam on toast.

After breakfast, we got dressed into our gym clothes for a session in the gym. After that, we had a warm shower to relax our muscles. We changed into our England strip and met the rest of the team in the hotel lobby. We all got on the coach and everyone was quiet.

After half an hour, we arrived at Liverpool Arena. I was starting to feel excited!

Our game started at 1pm. The seats were full and the atmosphere was epic! I played C and WA and I got 'Player of the Match'! The final score was 89-85. It was so close but we *won!*

We signed lots of autographs and took loads of selfies with the fans.

When we got back to the hotel, we had our late lunch and relaxed. We chatted about the game and how well we did.

Got to go now, need to pack up and get ready to leave on the coach to go home.

Darcey Batey (9)

The Incredible Diary Of... The Misunderstood Spider

Dear Diary,

I'm sick and tired of it, everybody scared of spiders but why? Oh, sorry! I've not introduced myself yet. I'm Sullivan, the misunderstood spider, and I live down here in the dark and dusty basement with nobody to talk to. I mean, us spiders have never done anything to hurt anybody except maybe a tarantula...

Thump, thump, thump! Creak!

"Arghh! That's a human! Oh no, I think she saw me."

"Hello little spider, don't be scared!" her voice as soft as snow.

I finally plucked up the courage to say, "Hi, what's your name?"

The girl gasped and lost all speech.

"Ruby," she stuttered. "Yours?" she said with a curious tone in her voice.

"Sullivan, but you can call me Sulli," I said.

"Do you want to be friends?" we said simultaneously.

70

Dear Diary,

It's a new day. "Morning," Ruby said to me as she crawled out of her pink kitten bed.

Once at school, Ruby took me to her playground to show me to her friends.

"Argh!" they shrieked louder than an actual fire alarm.

"There is nothing to be scared of!" replied Ruby.

Jasmine Wilkes (10)

The Incredible Diary Of... A Marvellous Day!

Dear Diary,

You will not believe what happened to me. It was Monday when this remarkable thing took place. I was watching the television. I felt petrified when the man on TV reported that five tigers were on the loose in town. Oh my god! This was a disaster! This was terrifying! What if they attacked people? What if they attacked me? They also said that the person who found even one of the tigers would get a reward! Since I was two years old, I've loved animals and tigers above all. So I decided to go on a tiger hunt.

Two hours passed and there was no sign. I was beginning to lose hope. Suddenly, out of the corner of my eye, I spotted something! Not one, not two but five!

"Oh no! Tigers!"

Just as I was about to scream my head off and run away, I remember what the man on TV said. As quick as a flash, I called the police and the RSPCA so they could catch them. Before I knew what was happening, the zookeeper came to me and gave me the reward. It was money. I felt very proud of myself but instead of keeping it, I gave it to the zoo.

From that time on, whenever I visit the zoo, I always remember to look at the tigers.

Aysha Afridi

The Incredible Diary Of... My Hero

Dear Diary,

Thursday, May 30th was a beautiful day in Richmond Park where I got to enjoy the beauty of nature and the beautiful houses with perfectly manicured lawns endorsed with beautiful flower gardens.

The people were ever so friendly. I remembered my mum said she visited over ten years ago and wanted to give me that wonderful exhilarating experience where they saw the deer in the wild. The day was glorious as I embraced the warm rays of the golden sunshine. After treading along the vast woodland of the park I watched the deer in their natural habitat, seeing the London Shard in the distance. The only sounds I could hear were the blackbirds chirping in the tall, green trees and the deafening sound of the aeroplane engines overhead.

Tired and feeling battered and hungry, I went to Pizza Express and gobbled down two margherita pizzas, one watermelon cooler and two apple and pear juices. The waiter then performed a magic trick.

Then, dragging my tired feet in my battered and worn shoes which unstuck in all the wrong places, I hobbled back to the train and made my way back into London...
It was so much fun.

Abigail Keen

The Incredible Diary Of...

Dear Diary,

Today I woke up hearing Ron snoring loudly (as usual) when I heard footsteps. They got louder and louder, until Professor Snape came with his unfriendly face inside the room.

"Good day, Potter," he said sternly as he carried on marching down the cold, dark corridor.

After he finally left, I got dressed into my dark robe and jumper and went to breakfast. Not surprisingly, I found Hermione sitting on a bench reading a spell book.

"What took you so long?" she finally said. "And where is Ronald?"

I didn't have time to answer because I was going to be late for spells with Professor Slughorn.

When I got there, Professor Slughorn was teaching the killing curse (this curse is not allowed to be taught to students but Professor Slughorn did it anyway).

"You're late again, Mr Potter!" he said, not surprised. "Third time this week!"

When spells was over, we had to go to a Quidditch match. My team won 180-30.

After that, we had dinner. Before I went to bed, I had to go see a new person who was joining Gryffindor. Then I went to bed.

Naomi Regha (9)

The Incredible Diary Of...

Dear Diary,

I watched the police lights illuminate the motorway whilst me and my grandson pulled the accelerator and darted down the motorway at seven miles per hour.

"Pull over with your hands up!" barked a man all of a sudden.

Slowly, I lowered my foot onto the brake and ushered Ben off the scooter.

"A ticket, ma'am," the officer explained, "for using your mobility scooter on this motorway! The second time this month, is it not?"

I explained, "It's the second Cling Film Society meeting in precisely thirty minutes, so we better be off."

He instructed, "That can wait! We are going to the police station!"

I felt my grandson's fingers shaking within mine. I realised I would have to take matters into my own hands.

"I could give you a 50% discount on cling film?" I said hopefully.

"Are you trying to bribe me, ma'am?" he bellowed.

Rapidly, I seized my grandson's hand and sprinted for my scooter. I rode away as fast as a tortoise, praying for the best. I was a criminal running away from the fuzz!

Emily Grace Parkinson (11)

The Incredible Diary Of... A Knight: A Not-So-Happily Ever After... After All!

Saturday 21st April, 849 AD
Day 42,
Dear Diary,
Currently, I happen to be in the palace dungeon. Unfortunately, I'm not the best knight when it comes to swordfights, and *crunch!* Ooh, that's definitely a concussion. How am I to save the princess now?

Saturday 21st April, 849 AD
Still Day 42
Dear Diary,
What a catastrophe! First, I had to escape the pitch-black prison I was put in, and luckily, I had just the right equipment. I looked at my fountain pen and it was the perfect shape for cutting through the shackles. I was almost there, I could feel it!
I made my way up towards the beautiful princess, opened the door, my head filled with excitement, then I realised something horrific had taken place!

The princess had her braid in hand, showing a sign of no-nonsense. Uh-oh.

She lashed out!

"Oww!" What do fair maidens put in their braids? Weights?

"I don't require rescuing from such arrogant knights! Leave!"

So, with all the weight of the world in my heart, I did. Unfortunately, it was not my destiny to rescue such a fine maiden from her tower of solitude...

Jia Vekaria (11)

The Incredible Diary Of... Ninja Nell

Dear Diary,

Ugh... another long day of work. Three rescues, no treats! Being a ninja is hard work, especially when your sidekick, Gallant Gwyn, caused one of the emergencies! I had to help a duck find its way back to the pond, get Gwyn out of that pond and then calm that duck down *again* because Gwyn scared the bark out of it! I'm in bed now, feasting on some chicken that was under the oven. Mmmm...

Anyway, let me tell you what happened yesterday. Oh... by the way, we're both dogs!

So it was a Fryday. Yes, I meant to spell it like that. Fryday is the day when my mum makes bacon! I jump on our stool and then I bound onto the counter. Next, I army-crawl under some cupboards and when I've finished, I chomp on that delicious bacon. Mmmm.... ahem. Sorry (again). What I didn't notice was a plump pigeon seemed to be glued to the fence.

Oh no! I thought. I scampered outside and ordered it to chew away the glue.

"Woof! Ruff!"

"Cooo!" the pigeon called as it flapped its wings and... flew away? I was super confused. Still, another successful rescue!

Niamh Cross (10)

The Incredible Diary Of... Sonic The Amazing Hedgehog

Dear Diary,

I am currently in Coconut Land, which is a weird-looking place where everything is either a coconut or made out of them. There is a legendary glowing coconut and no one knows how it got there or even what it does, however, nearly everyone knows exactly where it is, including myself.

One hour ago, eight robococomonkies were attacking me with gigantic coconuts. I felt incredibly angry, so angry that I wanted to use my hedgehog spikes and poke them! Unfortunately for me, they weren't sharp enough to obliterate them! Then I saw... *the legendary coconut!* All of a sudden, I had found myself running towards it and touching it. Apparently, it turns you into a coconut, though I wasn't quite certain that was true...

Then I saw the weirdest sight of my life. It was Egghead (Dr Eggman). He tried to fight me and I felt hopeless. I realised that all of his robomonkeys had turned into coconuts! The rest of his henchmen were not coconuts because they didn't touch the legendary coconut.

Suddenly, the ground shook and Eggman and I are now in the cocogalaxy on cocomoon.

Shreyan Patel (8)

The Incredible Diary Of...

Dear Diary,

I am Dale the chipmunk. I got this diary for my tenth birthday and it tells the story of my short but eventful life.

Today was my first day at Blackberry Prep. We've just moved from Belfast to London. My older brother, Chip, was trying to convince me that school was fun but as we got ready, I had a cunning trick up my sleeve. I 'couldn't' get the toothpaste out so Chip urged me to squeeze it harder. It was extremely full so when I squeezed it, it poured out like gooey slime all over him! I still had to go to school though...

The first lesson was PE. Everyone looked so mean and strong, I was petrified! I only had my Hollie (my old school) PE kit so I pretended that I was asthmatic.

I was distraught in front of the whole playground when I dropped my digestive biscuit. Then Chip was furious that his girlfriend had broken up with him so when he got home, he ripped out all of the photos of her from his album, and mine as he blamed me!

Tomorrow it's double French! Hopefully, I can impress Madame Dubois with my 'je ne sais quoi'!

Evie Marie Pearson (10)

The Moonlight Dream

Dear Diary,

Last night, something strange happened to me. I leapt out of bed to the window to feel the cold air rushing over my face and rustling my hair. With tremendous excitement, I sprung onto the windowsill and gazed at the full moon which seemed to be making me reckless and full of strangely giddy courage. Without a second thought, I bent my knees and jumped up, up, up! Down, down, down! Falling... falling... falling...

Heart hammering alarmingly in my chest, I gradually opened my eyes. The full moon was still bright and daring, millions of miles above. But instead of feeling moist green grass beneath my bare feet, grains of sand tickled my toes. Coming to my senses, I stood and stared at my surroundings. Wow! I was standing on a beach next to the ocean!

All of a sudden, out of the wild waves came one hundred dolphins. One came up to me. It was beckoning me. A few minutes later, I was riding over the waves contentedly on my new friend, feeling exhilarated.

This morning, I awoke at 7am, quite exhausted. Had I been dreaming? I found a salty puddle beside me...

Holly Dimery (10)

A Survivor's Daily Life

Dear Diary,

When I stirred my armour was dented and rusty. My sixteen eyelids parted, my amber pupils spinning in my sockets - I was awake?

The jungle had been destroyed, hopefully I searched for the scraps of a missile for breakfast, but none. The humans had cleaned up after this war. My human friend, Ali, the last of the Indians, said, "Do we have a plan?"

I said, "First, let's drink at the oasis."

The war of 3093 has just ended with few humans left on Earth. I am a science experiment gone wrong, a robotic creature of myth - a dragon-bot from an invading army of rogues hoping to destroy all humans.

Hopefully we (Ali and I) can save Earth.

Out of the ruined jungle into our secret bit of the desert, we went on our daily stroll to the oasis - a spiral pool with a bath in the middle.

On the way, we saw a small coconut palm, Ali bounded up for his lunch. I had to make do with two horseshoes that weren't too rusty.

At the oasis, we sat under the biggest, shadiest tree drinking. For me this means fuel, and Ali water, before bed.
Festus

Jessica Crisp (10)

The Incredible Diary Of... A Pencil

Dear Diary,

I have ultimately found a way out of the pencil box (my prison-like home) to write on this piece of paper with my own lead. Humans are nasty - stabbing us into paper and sometimes even piercing the paper! Especially those smaller, noisier ones that put us in backpacks and take us to school where I see other pencil boxes.

The taller, quieter humans always insisting on sharpening our heads, giving us headaches. I feel their heads should be sharpened too so that they can experience our pain and agony! I like humans more now they've left me behind. Three-month-old me has finally been left alone. The humans are returning, got to dash! Hope I will write in you soon.

From, the ordinary black and yellow pencil.

PS I might write in you soon. There are these new things called pens and more of them are entering the pencil box. Ever heard of anything called a 'fountain pen'?

More weird things are coming in, like pencils that smell from a company called Smiggle. It'll probably become a pen box soon and us pencils will be left alone. Hoorah!

Arna Kar (10)

The Incredible Diary Of... Lewis Hamilton

Dear Diary,

Today was the most shocking day of my life! Firstly, we had completed our training laps for our practise. Subsequently, the whistle went off to alert us to get ready to start the race. Soon, we were off and Sebastian was in the lead. I was tenth, speeding to ninth.

After a few laps, some of the cars crashed with tyres ripping and spoilers tearing, leaving 45 cars left in the race. I was sixth now and the laps were getting complicated.

"Arghh!" I shrieked.

A car was heading the wrong way and its driver with his hands in the air. What on earth was going on? Did he even have a license? Instantaneously, the car behind accelerated into me, leaving my tyres frayed. Still, I zoomed up to second position. It was getting intense now.

Two cars were millimetres behind me and a pigeon smashed onto my helmet. There were a few laps left but now the pigeon and I were face-to-face with Sebastian. We had to take a sharp left, leaving the side of my car with dents.

There were a few seconds left and he was leading. I accelerated and yes, I won!

Yusuf Aayan Kabir (11)

The April Fool's Day I Will Never Forget!

Dear Diary,

It's me again, same old Alison but in school, I'm known as Miss Marcy, although some of my students call me a monkey or a dinosaur and I end up having to send them to detention, thankfully it's only a few students that call me that. Anyways, today I went to school and I forgot that it was April Fool's Day! All the teachers are paranoid about this day and so am I!

I came into Class S2 and when I opened the door, a whole bucket of water plunged on me! *Freezing* cold! To make matters worse, one of the students took a photo and posted it on Instagram! Luckily, you couldn't see that it was me.

Since I was wet, I had to go change my clothes. *That* took me up until lunchtime (mainly because I took tremendously long to change). The next two classes weren't so bad but the last one was a nightmare!

When I went into Class S5 (the worst class in the entire school), they spat chewing gum on the ceiling and it fell into my hair! It took hours to take it out!

I hope that you had a better day than me, Diary. But, bye for now!

Marta Koziel (11)

The Incredible Diary Of... An Evacuee

Dear Diary,

I startled awake, seeing Mother sitting at the foot of my bed, her eyes red. She said good morning with a cheery voice but it was obvious that she wasn't happy about something. She passed me a tin saucer with a succulent piece of bacon and a glass of milk. I looked surprised. How could a middle-class family like us afford such a lavish meal? Seeing my astonishment, Mother told me to tuck in.

Soon, a lump of bacon got stuck in my throat and I knew why mother was acting so strangely. The thought hit me like a bullet. I was going to be evacuated. Streams of emotions washed over me like strong currents. I chewed my bacon but it didn't feel so fresh and succulent anymore. My eyes filled with tears at the thought of leaving my family just for the war effort. My vision blurred as something wet rolled down my cheek.

Suddenly, Mother passed me a dark navy book and on it was inscribed 'Diary'. My heart thumped as I received the small book into my hands.

I was going to be torn apart from my family.
Got to catch the train now, write soon.

Mariya Shiju

The Incredible Diary Of... My Squirrel Life

Dear Diary,

This morning I was awoken by my friends, Bobby, Billy and Shelly. They were dropping nuts on my head to wake me. I am a professional hide-and-seeker, so they woke me up to help them find Kelly, the baby squirrel of the family. We are city squirrels and we live in the central park. The baby was lost somewhere around town.

"Where did you last see her?" I questioned.

Without waiting for an answer, I continued, "Have you heard of the dog named Tim? He loves squirrels and sneaks around the park checking for them."

Just at that moment, I caught a glimpse of a black and white spotty tail, next to it was an orange bushy tail. I raced down the tree, hoping for the dog not to notice me and tugged the orange bushy tail. I raced back up the tree and discovered I had taken the dog's chew toy.

All of a sudden Kelly came out of her drey and asked, "What's that? It looks exactly like me!"

I smiled and dropped the chew toy out of the tree and went back into my drey to go back to bed. That was enough excitement!

Issy Mills (7)

The Stupidity That Led Me To Fame

Dear Diary,

Hi, I'm Alisha Azeem. I bought this diary to record precious memories as I forget a lot of things and also to look cool! Holding this in public makes me feel like Nikki J Maxwell from 'Dork Diaries', or Greg Heffley from 'Diary of a Wimpy Kid'.

In case you didn't know, I'm a superhero! But my power isn't any of the common ones like flying or invisibility. No, dude! I can see the *future!* Though I'm not that famous because, due to my power, I can only save people from undangerous situations, but today that all changed.

I had a vision that showed a girl dangling off a building! I stood there for four hours until I saw her. She raced towards me but I quickly moved as I thought that she was gonna push me! Then she fell off! I thought that she had died but she was holding onto the bricks! I quickly grabbed her arm before she lost grip. After that, I became *famous!* Everyone knew who I was but later on, I found out that the girl wanted a hug. She wasn't gonna push me, but no one knows about that.

Alisha Azeem

The Incredible Diary Of...

Dear Diary,

You will never believe my day - it was extraordinary! I was getting ready to go to the fair. I had been looking forward to it for months and I decided to borrow my sister's new cherry-pink lipstick. I was very careful that she wouldn't notice. Suddenly, my face started to puff up! It grew bigger and fatter! Peering into the mirror, I discovered that I had morphed into Kim Kardashian! I was in disbelief! I was in shock! I was speechless! What should I do? I had no option. I couldn't miss the fair, so I grabbed my headscarf as a disguise and headed off.

At the bus stop, my scarf blew off. Within seconds, my face was posted online! Soon, hoards of fans were shouting, "Kim! Over here!"

I was shoved about like a pink sock in a washing machine. Flashes blinded me, it was time to make the most of it so I struck a pose! I admit it, I loved it! But during one enthusiastic spin around, I accidentally caught someone on the nose! Luckily, I escaped in a limousine. I can't wait to see what happens when my sister wears the lipstick!

Maisie Fish

The Incredible Diary Of... Leena And The Romans

Dear Diary,

My name is Leena and I am nine years old and I live on the corner of Paragon Road. Today I fell through a purple, shiny door and entered a Minecraft dimension. I ran around for a while but then I found something on the ground. At first, I didn't know what it was but then...

I found out it was a Roman hat! Then I realised I was being watched and followed! That was when I knew the Romans were thinking of catching me! I felt scared and anxious.

Just then, I heard running and out of the blue, the Romans came charging right at me! I had to run but then I felt courageous and decided to fight back. I felt powerful because I fought those powerful Romans. Now there were no more! I had beaten them! How was I supposed to get home? I was scared because I wanted to get home! I stumbled into the wood to find some food.

Finally, I found some berries. I bent back a branch to get the berries but then a magical portal opened up from an old, forbidden tree. I hopped inside and the next thing I knew, I was back in my warm, cosy bedroom.

Georgia Russell

104

The Incredible Diary Of... Book World

Dear Diary,

I walked to school the other day. All as usual, but the thing was, I had a different morning. I went through a porthole in space and went through a land of books and they seemed to come alive. The pirate from 'Pirates Love Underpants' was zooming through the sky. Also, the ice monster from 'The Ice Monster' was storming about. Fing from 'Fing' was rolling around.

Finally, I landed in a book. It was 'Spider-Man'. I needed to get out of it so with the sticky spiderwebs, the Fing's hairs, the blink of an ice monster, I was off. Zooming through the sky again whilst meeting those book characters again. Some were boys, some were girls but I was still flying away.

In the end, I ran home to tell my mum and dad what a good day I had. Not at school, not at home, but flying through the blazing sky.

My mum said, "Well it's five o'clock. What a day you had zooming through that mind of yours!"

Okay, it's the end of the night so I wish you goodnight.

Jacob Swan (7)

The Incredible Diary Of... David And The Unicorn

Dear Diary,

Let me introduce myself, my name is David. Today was an awesome day, as I finally got my driving license for riding the unicorn that my dad bought me. Anyway, the day started with me waking up like a zombie and wearily demolishing my bowl of cereal. It was just an hour later when I started to freshen up like an angel, and I was looking at my diamond window like a hawk, waiting for my inspector to arrive.

At noon, the inspector arrived and he rang my doorbell, which made an ear-splitting noise that irritated me. I stood formally in front of the inspector and hopped on top of my unicorn, AJ, who has the skin of a glowing rainbow. I started to shiver with fear but I had to be confident at riding. On my wonderful journey, my eyes saw many diamond mansions; I also met my idol who was Ralph, the best unicorn rider ever.

In the end, it felt like I was frozen, and then I received my results... I *passed!*

It was like heaven filled with glory.

With happiness, I celebrated with an incredible party.
From David

Abishan Jesuthas

The Incredible Diary Of... My Hamster

Dear Diary,

We have just beaten Chelsea SC (Swimming Club) in the semi-finals! We were as fast as leopards and as excited as a baby with a new toy! This was so exciting! Our club has never been to the finals before. Next week, we play Man City in Birmingham. The match will be hard as Man City have won two times in a row.

Dear Diary,

It was the final. I climbed up onto the platform, ready to dive, arms in front of my head in lane two. Finally, after what I thought was ages, the whistle blew fiercely and I dived in, on I swam and on I raced. I felt like I was flying in the water. It was tense but I touched the solid wall at last. The man announced lane two first, one second, four third and three last. I actually beat one of the guys, I felt absolutely gobsmacked, this was a new record for us but not everyone was lucky, my friend, Dan, was in lane three.

After all the races were finished, the man announced that Man City had sixty-one points and we smashed them by seventy-eight!
Love Racy the hamster xxxxx

Jack Hei Lee (9)

Jeffery's Escape

Dear Diary,

I'm planning an escape to get out of French Fry prison back to Cheese Land. I'm in prison because I went to the car shop to buy a Cheeser. They didn't let me so I stole a Tesla model Cheese and they called 999 so now I'm in jail. At lunch, I'm going to eat through the fry wall, the cheese wall and then the jelly wall. When I encounter the five-armed, donkey-headed giant, there will be a sword in front of the jelly wall which I will fight with. Finally, I've finished packing and I'm about to go now.

Dear Diary,

I ate through the fry wall. It tasted so sweet and salty! Out of the corner of my eye, I saw an officer walk in and he saw me as I turned to eat more of the jelly and cheese wall. I darted to the acute, stinging, razor-sharp sword to slay the five-armed, donkey-headed giant but he was sleeping! Then I jumped in the Cheeser and zoomed home. I am now home and writing this diary because I want to remind myself to leave the Cheeser where it was.

Jake Canning (8)

One Of The Happiest Days Of My Life

Dear Diary,

Today our football team, Manchester United, beat Chelsea 6-5. Chelsea started with the ball. They played shockingly well, I have to admit. They scored three goals within about twenty minutes, while our team had two.

I had the ball and passed it to John, who passed it to Tony. I saw someone on the Chelsea team coming near Tony. I called out to Tony to pass the ball to me so the person on the Chelsea team did not get the ball.

Within a few minutes, I scored a goal. The whistle blew, which meant that the first half was over. This time we started with the ball. Jimmy had the ball but then he got tackled by someone on Chelsea. I was getting a little annoyed that Chelsea was beating us 5-4. Luckily, we caught up with them. I was running with the ball when suddenly, someone tackled me. I fell to the floor with a big loud thud.

A few minutes later, I woke up, only to find my team surrounding me. The coach said that it was a penalty. I decided to do a fake and scored a goal, again!

Abu Bakar Choudhry (9)

The Incredible Diary Of...

Dear Diary,

I am *so* proud of myself right now. I cannot believe I actually just sang in front of all those people! It was scary but fun all at the same time. You must know the feeling already though. Don't you remember the time I got you? Didn't *you* feel the same way? I guess not then. Maybe you were feeling more overjoyed than scared because someone finally picked you up and bought you. Anyways, I sang this one song and it was great. Plus, everybody loved it. However, the only problem was... it took me *ages* to get it right! Seriously, I am not exaggerating!

But I've got to say that, that was the most successful song I had ever sung. Maybe I could sing it to you sometime (by sing, I mean write). It's fabulous and it will also help me fill up the pages. Just keep thinking for me so I can know if I should hurt my fingers for you.

So that's it for now. Got to go, hope you're done thinking by the time I come back. Bye. Write to you later.

Chanelle Gatheru (11)

112

The Incredible Diary Of... A Sprinter

Dear Diary,

My name is Freya Hillsburg and today has to have been the most supreme day of my life! I had been counting down to this day more than my birthday. I woke up in the morning feeling like a different person. I didn't need to be reminded what was different. I popped out of bed like a toaster and realised it was the day of the big running event! Once I had finished my breakfast and had gathered all my water and snacks, I was ready to leave home when a terrible thought dawned on me. Last year, I came last in the race, yet I trained harder afterwards.

When I arrived at the sports stadium, there were lots of other runners too. We all chatted for about five minutes until a tall, thin, bony lady came and shouted at us to go and line up for the race.

As we lined up for the race, I started feeling nervous. A loud gun went off and we all ran. I was sprinting but couldn't see anybody on either side of me. Was I at the back or the front? I reached the end and I realised I had really won!

Anne-Marie Mensah (10)

The Incredible Diary Of... A Chicken Nugget

Monday, 12th July, 1964

Dear Diary,

There was a young boy called Tom. He had just passed his science exam. He was going home for dinner. On his plate, he saw a golden-brown chicken nugget, and that chicken nugget was me, Charles! He jabbed me in the tummy with the evil weapon of mystery - a fork! Then he cut me up with the guillotine of all food... a knife!

Then he picked me up and put me in his mouth. I dodged the death teeth which had edges like daggers, swung on the perilous uvula and jumped down into the stomach.

I landed on an old decrepit piece of pie. Picked up a choco-stick (a type of sweet) and rowed the pie across the acid lake. Eventually, there was a whirlpool and I got sucked in.

I woke up and found I had turned brown and I was in the smelly sewer. It had lots of exotic pongs, whiffs and even some odorous smells.

The only bad thing is that this place is home to lots and lots of mice, which terrify me!
Maybe I will have more adventures?

Henry de Bono (9)

The Incredible Diary Of... Leah

Dear Diary,

Today I went on holiday to a beach house. My room had a bed but also a wardrobe on the left. I thought the trip wasn't going to be fun. I was wrong! Once I'd played on the beach, I was so amazed that I didn't want to leave!

When I went inside, I started unpacking my clothes into the wardrobe. The wardrobe had a place to hang clothes and two drawers below it. Surprisingly, the upper drawer wasn't empty. Inside was a small, wooden box with a picture of a strange-looking cat carved on top. I was curious about what was inside. I unlatched the lock and it opened easily. Inside was a necklace with a charm that looked like a cat. I put it on...

Instantly it glowed. Then I wasn't in my room, I was on the beach. I saw a trail of glitter on the beach and I followed it. I saw a black cat with a unicorn horn! The cat shook its head and I was in my room again. I didn't know what had happened but soon I remembered so I started to write...

Saara Ahmed (8)

The Incredible Diary Of... Ayesha Holmes (AKA Sherlock Holmes)

Dear Diary,

Today I had an extremely strange thought. My pen scratched the homework book as I furiously scribbled: 'The Second World War started in 1939 and ended in 1945'. Mrs Bell then told us to finish writing our world war story and share our work.

As Thelma stood up, I gazed out of the window. Closing my eyes, I pictured the war and all the people fighting. How lucky we were, to be alive, not to have to be adopted by another family and start our lives from scratch. All our great grandparents had fought to save our lives. Our lives. To make life peaceful for us.

I was aware of everybody clapping as Thelma sat back in her seat. Mrs Bell searched the class and her eyes met mine.

"Ayesha, would you mind if we all listened to your story?"

My chair scraped the wooden floor. I walked up to the whiteboard, aware of 31 pair of eyes on me.

"It all began when the first siren started..."

Emily Charlotte Bussey (10)

The Incredible Diary Of... Lexi The Dog

Friday, 1st March 2019

Dear Diary,

This morning when I woke up, I sat in bed with Mummy. She always has her breakfast in bed. Emma the cat came in. I was worried she would get some of Mummy's breakfast! Luckily she didn't. Daddy took me for a walk on the Downs. I met my friend, Sadie. I was very excited to meet my friend, we ran round and round. I was very tired after my walk.

When I got home I had my chicken, then I had to have a bath. I didn't like my bath but I *did* like sitting on Tamsin's knee afterwards. She made me dry and I made her wet!

After lunch, I saw an intruder in the garden! I barked and frightened the bird away. I have to protect our other pets in the garden - the guinea pigs and chickens.

Tamsin went out tonight and I waited an hour and thirty-five minutes for her to come back! I played with my Heffalump toy until she finally came home.

Tamsin Lucy Wilcox

Unicorn Dreams

Dear Diary,

Today, I had loads of fun! I flew around a volcano and it didn't erupt! And when I flew to Crystal Cove, I found my unicorn friends waiting for me to celebrate my birthday (I thought I mentioned it was my birthday... did I?). Anyway, then we went to the Tumbling Tower and started digging at the spot where we found the X mark. Boring part was that we found... nothing. That's it.

Oh! For my birthday, I got new powers for my horns, which were... umm... oh yeah! It was reading other unicorns' minds. Well... it isn't really a power. It is actually a privilege! Now, I am allowed to fly around to distant galaxies by myself! Usually we have to go with some adult unicorn. It was the *best gift* ever from my mummy unicorn and daddy unicorn.

Aparajita Bajpai (8)

The Story Of A Squirrel

Dear Diary,

Today I had just been chilling in my tree but my wife had been nagging me to get this new car but I didn't really want to because I had money but then we would have no money. I hoped she wouldn't leave me for Larry with the fluffy tail because if she did, it'd be over for me. Then she called me. She took the kids and she said, "It's over!"

Then I said, "Fine, are you leaving me for that idiot, Larry?"

"Yes! Say bye to the kids, sorry!"

I ran and ran but what I did not see there was a car. Then all of a sudden, I saw my kids and my wife, even Larry, and I was in a hospital bed hearing *beep, beep, beep*. Then the doctor said, "He'll never walk again."

Louis Harry David Adams (10)

The Incredible Diary Of...

Dear Diary,

My name is Ariana Grande. Today I sang my new song. It was so much fun. It is called '7 Rings'. I sang it in my music video but today, I sang it live on stage. Lots of my friends and family were there. Also, my fans! They all screamed, "I love you, you're the best!" Some were singing along! I think it is one of my best songs I have ever sung. My favourite part of the song is the first part. It was a bit hard to sing but in the end, I did it. It took lots of practice to do. All of the backup dancers did very well too. In the end, everyone did well, even the audience!

At the end, we celebrated because we had finally finished the show and everyone was happy. That was the end of my day.

Lillymay Walsh-Pierce (9)

An Extraordinary Friday

Dear Diary,

When I went to the library yesterday morning to pick up a book, I was looking at some history books when I saw a tall girl with light brown hair and she had a stripy bag. I crept towards the bag to see what was inside it, but all of a sudden, she turned around. I got a little glance at what was inside, there were lots of books.

Then I realised she must be a book thief!

That night, I watched her creep out of the library with lots of books in her bag. I snuck towards her, but she swung round at that moment. She shone her torch at me and screamed, "Aargh!"

Then she tried running away but I caught her and advised her that it was not good to steal books from the library.

Aasiyah Razzaq

The Incredible Diary Of...

Dear Diary,

Adults are so weird, like seriously! When my siblings are at school, my mum pressures me to say 'Mama' and when my dad comes back from work it's the same thing, but he tells me to say 'Dada'.

Earlier, I just didn't know what to do so I decided to copy my mum and suddenly, everyone started screaming! Why? In addition to that, they keep on trying to make me walk and it's been going on for about a month so when I actually walked, they started flashing lights which made me fall on my face! They're out to get me!

Have to go. My milk is ready and then I have to go to bed. They treat me like a baby!

Hajra Jamshed (10)

The Incredible Diary Of...

Dear Diary,

The other day, I had the worst day ever! Everyone was shouting at me until I decided to go to my room but then I started talking to my budgie about what happened. Suddenly, my budgie, Zach, started to reply back to me. I was shocked about what happened. After we chatted, it was time to eat and all the things I didn't like, I gave to Zach. The next day, Zach wasn't talking because everything was okay. Then I realised when good things happen, Zach doesn't talk and when something bad happens, he talks.

Sayf Mushtaq

Open Your Eyes

I am a lonely tree. All my friends used to stand right next to me, but not anymore. We used to talk and laugh and sing and play but those days are long gone. Humans are the problem, they cut us and smash us and break us to pieces even though we don't harm them. We actually help them. We shade them and protect them just like a mum and they still do nothing except harm us. But we have a life too, so wake up and start treating us with a kind heart. Us trees would like some more friends.

Rithika Raghunandanan (9)

Young Writers Information

We hope you have enjoyed reading this book – and that you will continue to in the coming years.

If you're a young writer who enjoys reading and creative writing, or the parent of an enthusiastic poet or story writer, do visit our website **www.youngwriters.co.uk**. Here you will find free competitions, workshops and games, as well as recommended reads, a poetry glossary and our blog. There's lots to keep budding writers motivated to write!

If you would like to order further copies of this book, or any of our other titles, then please give us a call or order via your online account.

Young Writers
Remus House
Coltsfoot Drive
Peterborough
PE2 9BF
(01733) 890066
info@youngwriters.co.uk

Join in the conversation!
Tips, news, giveaways and much more!

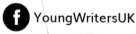 YoungWritersUK @YoungWritersCW